THE DRAGON'S ROBE

Deborah Nourse Lattimore

HarperTrophy
A Division of HarperCollins Publishers

In loving memory of
Eleanor Lattimore Andrews

The Dragon's Robe
Copyright © 1990 by Deborah Nourse Lattimore
Printed in Mexico. All rights reserved.

Library of Congress Cataloging-in-Publication Data
Lattimore, Deborah Nourse.
   The dragon's robe / Deborah Nourse Lattimore.
      p.   cm.
   Summary: A young weaver in twelfth-century China saves her people
from drought and foreign invasion by weaving the imperial dragon's robe.
   ISBN 0-06-023719-8. — ISBN 0-06-023723-6 (lib. bdg.)
   ISBN 0-06-443321-8 (pbk.)
   [1. China—Fiction.]   I. Title.
PZ7.L.36998Dr   1990   89-34512
[E]—dc20   CIP
                                                                AC

Typography by Andrew Rhodes
First Harper Trophy edition, 1993.

ABOUT THE DRAGON'S ROBE

In China for many centuries the dragon was believed to be the king of the heavens and ruler of fortune on earth. People stopped at the small shrines that dotted the countryside and made offerings to the dragon in exchange for good luck. Even the emperor had a dragon crown, a dragon throne, and a dragon robe called a Chi Fu. Whenever he wore his Chi Fu, the emperor and the dragon became one power. Together they were responsible for the safety of China and all its people.

The emperor in this story is Hui Tsung, the last ruler of the Northern Sung dynasty, which ruled from the tenth century to the thirteenth century A.D. He loved painting and poetry and neglected his other duties. During his reign he stayed in his palace and sent his nobles to pay the warlike Tartar tribesmen in order to keep them from invading. When a drought ruined the rice crops, Hui Tsung continued to paint. He sent more nobles to inspect the land, but his messengers weren't honest, and the work was never done. Hungry for Chinese riches, the Tartars invaded, and the Emperor was taken prisoner. Kao Tsung, the Emperor's son, escaped to the south and set up a new palace at Hangchou.

I named the weaver Kwan Yin after the goddess of mercy, who appears in every dynasty of Chinese art. The paintings of the Northern and Southern Sung dynasties are especially noted for their rich, calm landscapes. When we look at these pictures, it is hard to imagine the turbulent times that produced them.

D.N.L.

There was once a girl named Kwan Yin whose parents had died when she was young, leaving her nothing but a small loom. Kwan Yin became a skilled weaver, traveling from village to village, weaving in exchange for her meager food and a place to lay her sleeping mat.

The time came when there was no work to be found. Kwan Yin looked to the mountains beyond the Hwang Ho River and said to herself, "The Emperor's palace at Kaifeng has work and food for all. I will make my fortune there." She tied her loom to her back and climbed the path.

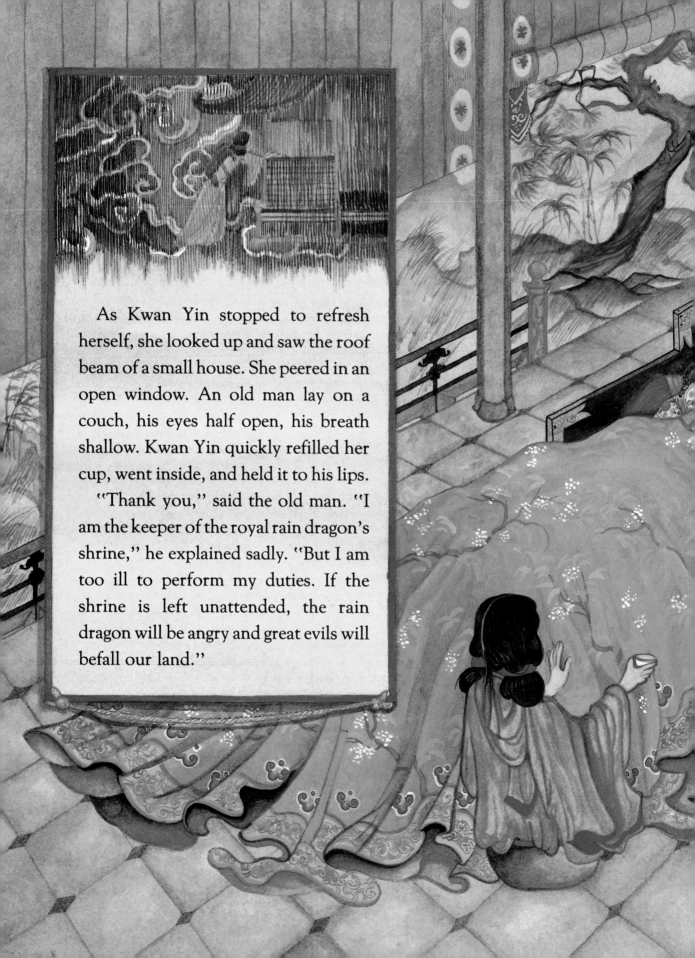

As Kwan Yin stopped to refresh herself, she looked up and saw the roof beam of a small house. She peered in an open window. An old man lay on a couch, his eyes half open, his breath shallow. Kwan Yin quickly refilled her cup, went inside, and held it to his lips.

"Thank you," said the old man. "I am the keeper of the royal rain dragon's shrine," he explained sadly. "But I am too ill to perform my duties. If the shrine is left unattended, the rain dragon will be angry and great evils will befall our land."

"I am a poor weaver with no home and no family," replied Kwan Yin. "But I have heard that the Emperor has offered a reward for anyone who can weave the great dragon robe. I have only three days to get to the palace of Kaifeng, but I will pass your shrine on the way. Perhaps I can help."

"Then stay here for a day," said the old man. "Already with your company I feel stronger. And you will weave a better robe on a full stomach."

Kwan Yin felt sorry for the old man. Besides, in all her wanderings no one had freely offered her food and a place to sleep. So she stayed.

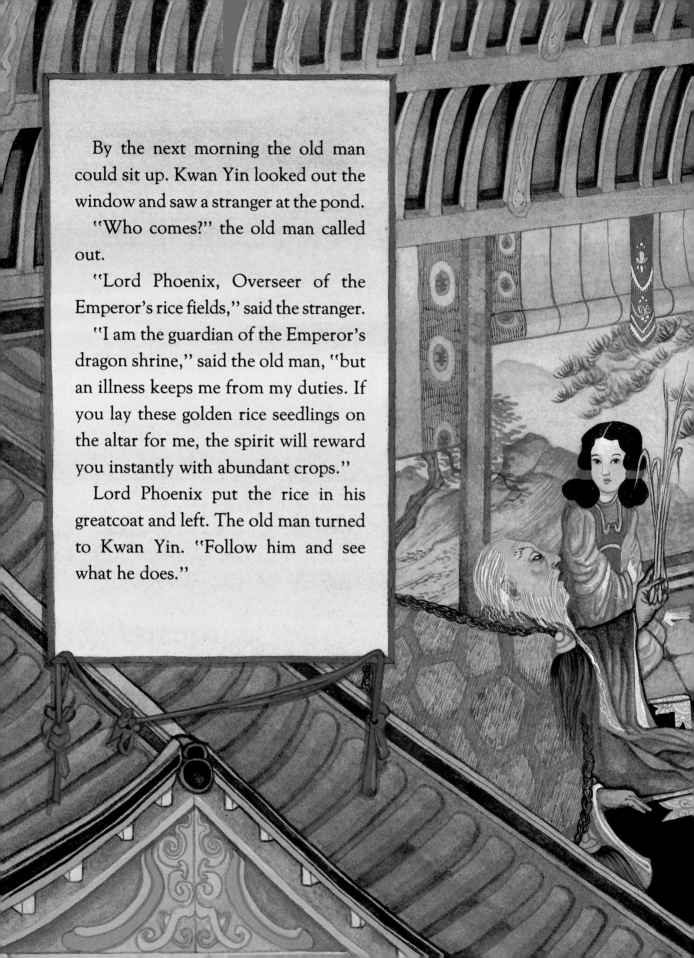

By the next morning the old man could sit up. Kwan Yin looked out the window and saw a stranger at the pond.

"Who comes?" the old man called out.

"Lord Phoenix, Overseer of the Emperor's rice fields," said the stranger.

"I am the guardian of the Emperor's dragon shrine," said the old man, "but an illness keeps me from my duties. If you lay these golden rice seedlings on the altar for me, the spirit will reward you instantly with abundant crops."

Lord Phoenix put the rice in his greatcoat and left. The old man turned to Kwan Yin. "Follow him and see what he does."

Then he went to sleep and Kwan Yin, followed Lord Phoenix, ten steps behind.

When the Overseer reached the shrine, he examined the golden seedlings from end to end.

"Never have I seen such wondrous golden rice!" he said to himself. "It would be foolish to leave it here for the dragon spirit, and besides, the Emperor is a fool who does not leave his palace. He will never know."

Lord Phoenix slipped the seedlings back into his greatcoat and went on his way to Kaifeng.

Kwan Yin returned, worrying that the news would upset the old man. But before she could speak, the air churned into a simmering wind and the rice fields for miles around burned to dust.

Kwan Yin decided to stay another night. On the second day the old man was indeed better, and with Kwan Yin's help he took small steps around his house. Suddenly the door burst open with a blast of hot wind. There stood another stranger.

"I am Lord Tiger," he announced, "General of the Emperor's army on the Great Wall. I must have drink, and the drought has dried up your pond."

Kwan Yin scooped up a cup of water from the bucket in the doorway and gave it to him.

"Great lord," said the old man, "I am the guardian of the Emperor's dragon shrine, but an illness keeps me from my duties. If you lay this golden knife on the altar, the spirit of the rain dragon will swiftly reward your army with victory in battle."

Lord Tiger put the knife in his cloak and left. Again the old man said to Kwan Yin, "Follow him and see what he does." Then he lay down to sleep.

Kwan Yin followed Lord Tiger, ten steps behind, until they reached the shrine. Lord Tiger took out the knife.

"Never have I seen such a magnificent golden knife!" Lord Tiger said aloud. "Why leave such a gift here when I can have it for myself? The dragon spirit will not miss it, and the Emperor, who values only the courtly life of his palace, will never know."

So he put the knife back in his cloak and went on his way.

Kwan Yin returned, wondering how to tell the old man what she had seen. But before she could speak, the distant thunder of horses' hooves and the cries of warriors came from the Great Wall.

"What I feared has come true," said the old man, standing at the window. "The General and the Overseer have dishonored the shrine. Now all China suffers from their evil deeds. Look how the crops wither! Our Tartar enemies and their cruel chief, the Khan, ride to attack us!"

The old man lay back on his couch.

"I am neither farmer nor soldier," Kwan Yin said to him. "I cannot sow new rice fields, and I cannot fight the Tartars. But I can weave a robe fit for the Emperor himself and lay it before the shrine of the rain dragon."

"Then go," said the old man. "Perhaps a humble weaver can undo the insults of the Overseer and the General. Let nothing stop you. The dragon spirit will help."

Kwan Yin took her loom and set to work.

Suddenly Lord Phoenix appeared on the path. He planted his feet beside Kwan Yin's loom.

"Move over!" he ordered. "Our people are fleeing the drought lands and you are in our way!"

Kwan Yin silently continued weaving.

"I command you to stop!" Lord Phoenix cried, and put his hand on her shoulder.

The golden rice seeds fell from his greatcoat. The spirit of the rain dragon cast them to the ground. Like firecrackers they exploded. A raging circle of flame and smoke engulfed the Overseer. In the instant the fire died out, a brilliant phoenix flew from the ash and was gone forever.

Kwan Yin continued weaving, though the flames had singed her fingertips. The sleeves of the great robe flew in the breeze and the back panels with their dragon scales rose in the warp.

Then, with a deafening clatter, Lord Tiger and his men mounted the path.

"Leave this place!" shouted Lord Tiger. "Already the Khan and his Tartar army have scaled the Great Wall. We are in full retreat!"

Kwan Yin heard his words and wove faster and faster. *Whirrrr*, sang her shuttle as it crossed the silken weft.

"Stop!" shouted Lord Tiger, reaching out.

The golden knife slipped from his coat. The spirit of the rain dragon cast it to the ground. Its splinters sprang up into a grove of trees that surrounded the General and his horse. In a flash, a tiger clawed its way up and over the smallest boughs and fell off into the valley below, and vanished forever.

Kwan Yin wove as never before. With four more layers of silk, the robe would be finished.

Moments later swirling clouds of dust rolled across the path and the great Khan himself appeared.

"Stand in my presence!" the great Khan said.

One, two, three times Kwan Yin wove the silk. The Khan grabbed her arm. Kwan Yin gave the shuttle its final toss. The robe was complete.

"Ah! The Imperial robe!" exclaimed the Khan. "Since I soon will be Emperor, it belongs to me. Move back!"

With that, the Khan gripped the hem and shook the robe with all his might to air it out before he put it on.

The robe unfurled against the door of the shrine. Its sleeves lashed out at the altar while the Khan struggled to pull it back.

Suddenly the spirit of the rain dragon filled the skies. In a single razor stroke it snatched the robe and took the Khan along with it. Its gaping mouth unleashed an ocean of whirling rainwater. Over the mountain it washed and flooded the valley. Not a single enemy warrior remained.

Kwan Yin drank in the fresh air. Her fingers were whole and mended. Instead of her poor, tattered garments, she found herself arrayed in the finest silk. Below her on the path stood the old man, his arms outstretched, in a dazzling golden robe.

"*You* are the Emperor!" Kwan Yin said.

"Yes," replied the old man. "And a wiser one, too. Before, I lived contentedly in my palace. I trusted my rich nobles, who told me only what I wanted to hear. But a poor weaver has taught me that true honor and goodness can come only from honesty and hard work, not flattery and lies. Will you come live in my palace, Kwan Yin, and help me remember what I have learned?"

Kwan Yin smiled. The gift of the rain dragon shone in her eyes.